Hall of Fame Sports Greats

DEION SANDERS

Hall of Fame Football Superstar

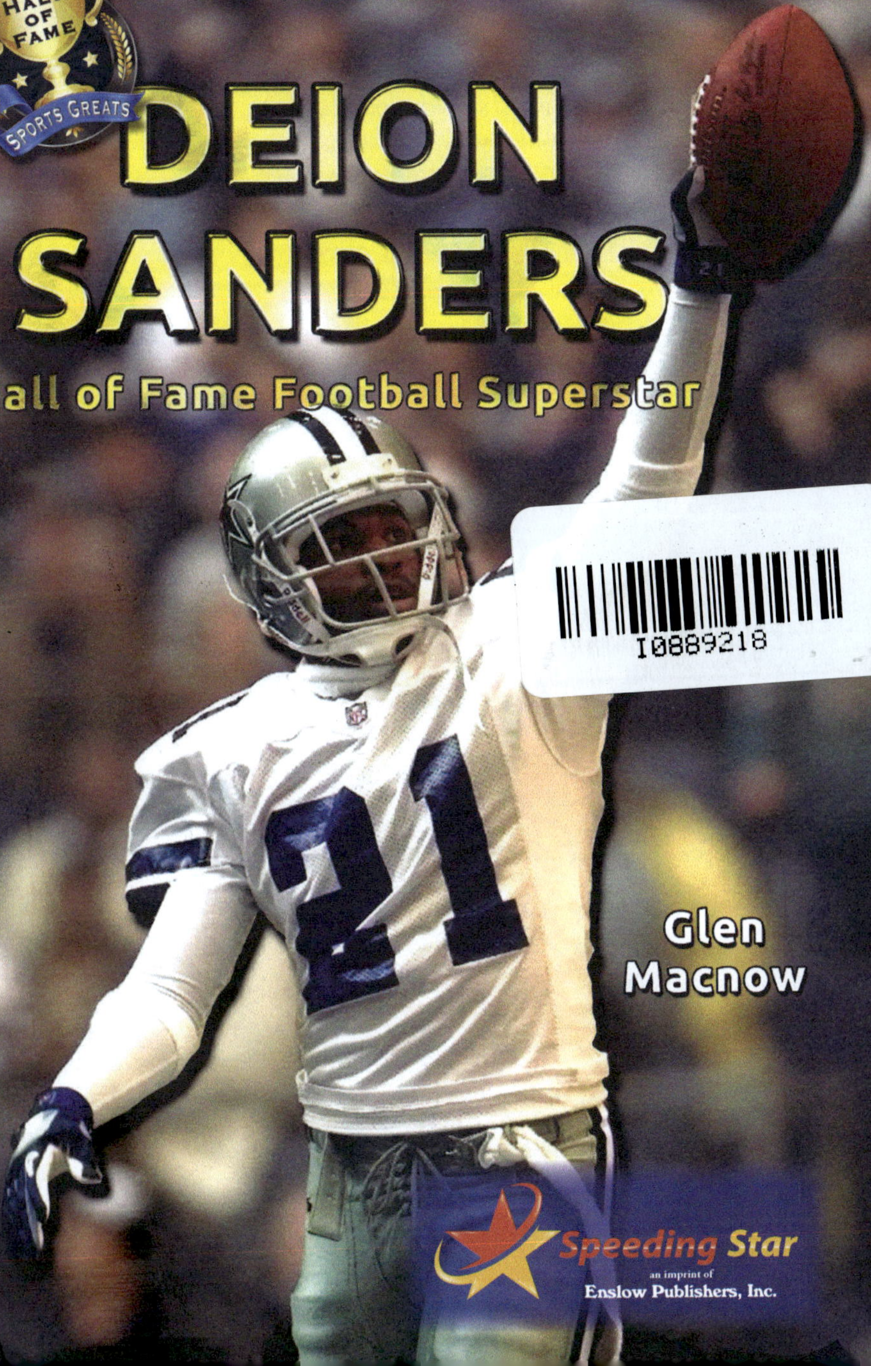

Glen Macnow

Speeding Star
an imprint of
Enslow Publishers, Inc.

This title was originally published in 1998 as *Sports Great Deion Sanders*

Speeding Star, an imprint of Enslow Publishers, Inc.

Library of Congress Cataloging-in-Publication Data

Macnow, Glen.
Deion Sanders : hall of fame football superstar / Glen Macnow.
pages cm. — (Hall of fame sports greats)
Includes bibliographical references and index.
Summary: "Read about Hall of Fame football player Deion Sanders in this sports biography. Follow Deion through his career that went from his childhood struggles to playing professional baseball and football to becoming one of the most legendary and flashy Hall of Fame football players ever."
—Provided by publisher.
ISBN 978-1-62285-045-7 (alk. paper)
1. Sanders, Deion—Juvenile literature. 2. Football players—United States—Biography—Juvenile literature. I. Title.
GV939.S186M32 2013
796.332092—dc23
[B]

2012043120

Future Editions:
Paperback ISBN: 978-1-62285-046-4
EPUB ISBN: 978-1-62285-048-8
Single-User PDF ISBN: 978-1-62285-049-5
Multi-User PDF ISBN: 978-1-62285-152-2

Printed in the United States of America

042013 Lake Book Manufacturing, Inc., Melrose Park, IL

10 9 8 7 6 5 4 3 2 1

To Our Readers: We have done our best to make sure all Internet addresses in this book were active and appropriate when we went to press. However, the author and the Publisher have no control over, and assume no liability for, the material available on those Internet sites or on other Web sites they may link to. Any comments or suggestions can be sent by e-mail to comments@speedingstar.com or to the address listed below:

Speeding Star
Box 398, 40 Industrial Road
Berkeley Heights, NJ 07922
USA
www.speedingstar.com

Photo Credits: AP Images/Alex Menendez, p. 12; AP Images/David Banks, p. 6; AP Images/Doug Mills, p. 38; AP Images/Ed Reinke, p. 49; AP Images/Eric Risberg, p. 45; AP Images/G. Newman Lowrance, p. 58; AP Images/Greg Trott, p. 27; AP Images/Joe Holloway, Jr., p. 35; AP Images/John Bazemore, p. 47; AP Images/LM Otero, p. 1; AP Images/Michael Mulvey, p. 56; AP Images/Mike Poche, p. 40; AP Images/Paul Jasienski, p. 4; AP Images/Paul Spinelli, pp. 22, 25; AP Images/Raul De Molina, 15; AP Images/Richard Drew, p. 29; AP Images/Ron Frehm, p. 20; AP Images/Tim Sharp, p. 54.

Cover Illustration: AP Images/LM Otero

CONTENTS

Deion Sanders is one of the best defenders to ever play football. He was referred to as a two-way threat because he excelled at both defense and offense.

Chapter 1

The Early Years

For years, Deion Sanders was called pro football's ultimate two-way player. Here is an example why:

Go back to January 7, 1996 when Sanders and the Dallas Cowboys were hosting the Philadelphia Eagles in a National Football League playoff game. Sanders, normally a cornerback, was pulling double duty by also playing wide receiver that day. In the second quarter, Cowboys coach Barry Switzer decided to take advantage of Sanders's speed by handing him the ball on a double reverse. Sanders electrified the Texas Stadium crowd by running 21 yards for Dallas's first touchdown.

Later in the same game, Sanders caught a key pass for 13 yards. He returned two punts for another 21 yards. And with

Deion Sanders waits to hear his name called during the 1989 NFL Draft. He was flashy even before he was a superstar. Sanders once said, "If you look good, you feel good. You feel good, you play good. You play good, they pay good!"

Philadelphia driving in the fourth quarter, he stepped in front of Eagles receiver Fred Barnett to intercept a pass and clinch the playoff win.

Three weeks later, the Cowboys beat the Pittsburgh Steelers in Super Bowl XXX. Sanders chipped in on defense with a pass deflection. He helped on offense by hauling in a 47-yard bomb from quarterback Troy Aikman that set up a touchdown. Then he joined his teammates in celebrating their world championship.

"Deion has meant so much to this club that I could speak for hours and not list it all," Cowboys owner Jerry Jones said afterward. "On defense, he's the best cornerback in the NFL. On offense, he's an extremely dangerous man. And on special teams, he throws fear into the other team. I see him as a three-way weapon."

Two-way weapon? Three-way weapon? Deion Sanders was more like a ten-way weapon. As he carved out careers in football and baseball in the 1990s, Sanders did things that men before him only dreamed of.

Only a small number of athletes have ever played two professional sports. Few of them could really boast of being a success at both. But Sanders can. He is the only athlete in history to star in both a World Series and a Super Bowl. In fact, he wears two Super Bowl rings—one for the Cowboys and one for the San Francisco 49ers.

In 1992 he became the only player ever to suit up for teams in two different sports on the same day. He played an afternoon football game with the Atlanta Falcons. That night, he dressed for the Atlanta Braves major-league baseball playoff game.

In baseball, Sanders was a center fielder and feared leadoff hitter. He once led the league in triples and was always among the league leaders in stolen bases.

In football, he was even more feared. Some consider him the best one-on-one cover man in history. Although he was small by NFL standards—just 195 pounds when he played—he was durable enough to be the first man in more than ten years to start for his team on both offense and defense. Sanders had even managed to score touchdowns six different ways—by running the ball, catching a pass, recovering a fumble, and returning kickoffs, punts, and interceptions.

He may have been pro sports' most colorful athlete. In fact, Sanders was so flashy that he required two nicknames—Neon Deion and Prime Time. He still prefers the second name. His brash style, his loud clothing, and his pounds of gold jewelry had earned him the love of some fans and the scorn of others.

Sanders recognized this and defended his image. "If you look good, you feel good," he once said. "You feel good, you play good. You play good, they pay good."

Besides, he says, people who judge him on appearance are making a mistake. On the outside he may have been flashy. On the inside, he says, he is still the same young man who grew up straight in a tough neighborhood in Fort Myers, Florida.

Sanders was born on August 9, 1967. His mother, Connie Sanders, wanted a special name for her first child. She came up with Deion Luwynn Sanders.

Deion was raised in a modest housing project on Anderson Avenue in Fort Myers. His father, Mims Sanders, and Deion's mother were separated soon after Deion's birth. Meanwhile, Connie Sanders worked two jobs to feed and clothe her son. When Deion was seven, his mother married Willie Knight. Together, they had two daughters, and the family moved a few blocks into a small house.

It was a tough neighborhood. Drug dealers sold their poison right on the streets. At night, Deion would hear gunshots in the distance. He would get headaches from the stress. An older neighbor whom Deion admired was sent to jail for selling drugs. He warned Deion not to follow his dead-end example. This young boy listened, but others did not. "My childhood friends, all of my boys," he once said, "ninety percent of them are in jail doing time for drugs."

Deion's escape from hard times was always sports. He started playing T-ball—baseball for beginners—at age five. His mom would rush over from her cleaning job at the hospital to cheer for her son. From the start, he was the fastest boy on the team. In fact, he stole bases so often that an opposing manager asked for a rule change putting a limit on any player's steal attempts.

At age eight, Deion joined a Pop Warner League football team. He soon scored his first touchdown, which came on a punt return. And the first touchdown led to his first touchdown dance. "I was so excited that when I got to the end zone I did some stupid little step," he said. "Everyone laughed."

In Deion's three years with the Fort Myers Rebels, the team won 38 games and lost just one. In 1979, the Rebels won a national Pop Warner football championship. Deion played quarterback on offense, and cornerback on defense. He scored an incredible 120 touchdowns in those 39 games.

His heroes back then were all athletes. On his bedroom wall there were posters of football's Lynn Swann, baseball's Hank Aaron, and basketball's Julius Erving. His favorite of all, however, was boxing champion Muhammad Ali. That made sense; Ali was the ultimate showman. He was a brash-talking, flashy-dressing superstar who knew that a big part of sports was show business. "I loved Ali as a kid," Sanders said as an adult. "I was always in love with the whole idea of Ali." No surprise, then, that the skinny little boy would grow up to go on a similar quest for celebrity and fame.

By the time he entered North Fort Myers High School, Deion was tall—nearly six feet—but weighed just 130 pounds. "Deion was the skinniest, shrimpiest little kid you would ever want to see," said high school football coach Wade Hummel. "He was a good athlete, with a feisty attitude. But he was just so skinny. We thought he was too small to help our varsity team."

It didn't take long, however, for the skinny kid to contribute. As a sophomore, he practiced with the team but never played. As a junior, he played cornerback. As a senior, he was a left-handed quarterback in a wishbone offense. He passed for 839 yards and ran for 499 more.

Deion starred for the high school baseball team, stealing 24 bases as a senior. He was drafted by the Kansas City Royals in the sixth round, but turned down their offer. He was also a sprinter and hurdler on the track team. His best sport, however, was basketball. He was a point guard who averaged 24 points a game as a senior. It was Deion's talent at dunking a basketball—not running a football—that earned him the nickname Prime Time.

"When he was in high school, I don't think he ever had it in his mind to be in the NFL or play pro baseball or anything like that," said Bobbie Dewey, North Fort Myers High's athletic director. "What everyone loved about Deion is that he played sports for the sheer love of it, for the thrill of it. Before basketball games, he'd entertain people. He'd stand flat-footed under the basket with a ball in each hand. Then he'd leap into the air and dunk both balls, one after the other, like he was hanging in the air defying gravity. The fans would just go nuts when he did that."

Shortly before graduating, Sanders was named High School Athlete of the Year by the *Fort Myers News-Press.* He had made the all-state teams in both basketball and football. And, of course, there was that baseball offer from the Royals, who happened to be his favorite team.

There were other offers. Dozens of colleges offered him scholarships to play football or basketball for their teams. Deion decided he would focus on football. He weighed just 140 pounds at age seventeen, but he had blinding speed and great determination.

He sorted through all the scholarship offers and narrowed his choices to four schools: Florida State University, the University of Miami, the University of Florida, and the University of South

Deion Sanders was a high school football star, and so is his son, Deion, Jr. Sanders, Jr., chose to attend Southern Methodist University. Deion, Sr., coached his son during the 2012 Under Armour All-America High School Football Game.

Carolina. His mother asked him to forget about Carolina. She did not want him to leave his native state.

Deion visited the three other schools. Then he announced his choice. He would attend Florida State University. The key to his decision was FSU coach Bobby Bowden. The nationally respected coach promised to give Deion a chance to play in his freshman year.

So in the fall of 1985, Deion Sanders registered as a freshman in college. He was handed some textbooks and the football jersey number two. He would not start at defensive back as a freshman, but he would see some game action.

Soon it became apparent that he would make the most of that chance.

Chapter 2

College Years

Truth be told, Florida State University was not interested in Deion Sanders at first.

Assistant Coach Mickey Andrews scouted Deion as a high school player. What Andrews first noticed was a left-handed quarterback leading a running offense. That did not fit FSU's offense at all. Months later, however, Andrews watched Deion play in a high school basketball game.

"He was a sensational shooter and a good defensive player," Andrews said. "But what absolutely amazed me was his ability to stop and go, to turn and move without the ball. He would backpedal down the court to cover a fast break quicker than most men could run forward. He had great peripheral vision.

I'm sitting there on the bench and I tell myself I'm not seeing a kid play basketball. I'm seeing a kid play defensive back in football. He had all the moves."

Sanders did not start as a college freshman, but he did get playing time. In a game against Tulsa University, he intercepted a pass on his goal line and sprinted 100 yards—untouched—for a touchdown. Head Coach Bobby Bowden liked the way Sanders handled the ball, so Bowden assigned him to return punts. Against the University of Florida, Sanders lived up to his Prime Time nickname. He caught a punt at his own 42-yard line. Then, in heavy traffic, he bobbed left, darted to the right,

Deion, wearing No. 2, is shown here with Bob Hope and the other 1988 All-Americans. NFL scouts, as well as MLB scouts, were already talking about how he could be a star in either sport.

faked three men off their feet, and returned the ball all the way. It was the first of 6 punt returns he would take for touchdowns during his four years as a Florida State Seminole.

Coach Bowden admired Sanders's talent. And the coach loved his young player's work ethic. "He was a good kid from a good home," Bowden said. "Very attached to his mother. He listened to everything coaches told him. He studied football like it was science."

That season ended with a 34–23 win over Oklahoma State University in the Gator Bowl. Sanders helped with an interception and six tackles. But his freshman athletic year was far from over. When his football teammates began spring drills, Sanders was playing right field for FSU's baseball team. He batted .333 with 11 steals in 16 games. His season ended early when he sprained his ankle.

As a college sophomore, Sanders moved into the football team's starting lineup. He quickly drew notice for his incredible speed and on-field smarts. At season's end he was named the Most Valuable Player on FSU's defense and was chosen for four All-America teams.

There were highlights galore. One of the best came in a loss to the University of Miami Hurricanes. Miami quarterback Vinny Testaverde and wide receiver Michael Irvin—two future NFL stars—faked out Sanders on a stop-and-go pattern. As Sanders bit on the fake, Irvin broke upfield. Testaverde threw as deep as he could to what seemed to be a wide-open receiver. But somehow, Sanders recovered. He caught up with Irvin and leaped over Irvin's shoulder to intercept the pass. Coach

Bowden said it was the best catch he had seen since the famous "basket catch" in baseball's 1954 World Series. "He looked like Willie Mays making that over-the-shoulder catch," Bowden said.

Sanders again played baseball during his sophomore year. In fact, he was offered a contract to turn pro by the Kansas City Royals. He quickly turned that down because he was having too much fun in college. He enjoyed the challenge of being a two-sport star.

As challenges go, he accepted a near-impossible one on a spring weekend in 1987. Sanders and his FSU baseball teammates had traveled to South Carolina to play in a tournament. They had a doubleheader that Sunday. Before the first game started, however, FSU track coach Dick Roberts, whose team was in town for a tournament of its own, came to Sanders with a problem. Roberts's top sprinter and hurdler, Arthur Blake, had a sudden case of the flu. The track team was short a runner for its 4 X 100-meter relay race. Sure, the coach said, Sanders had never run track, but he was the fastest man on the FSU campus. Would he consider filling in for Blake?

Sanders, with his baseball coach's approval, quickly agreed. So the stage was set for an incredible one-day performance.

At 3:00 P.M., Sanders played in the day's first baseball game. He doubled and scored a run. The Seminoles beat Mississippi University. Then, as his baseball teammates showered, Sanders changed from baseball spikes to track spikes. Wearing a track shirt and his baseball pants, he ran the second leg of the race. He almost dropped the baton, but finished his leg in 10.3

seconds—an outstanding time. The Seminoles placed second in the race. That helped them win the day's tournament.

As soon as the race ended, Sanders sprinted back to the baseball field. He got there as the national anthem was playing. In the sixth inning, he smacked a bases-loaded single to win the game against the University of Cincinnati Bearcats. For the second time that day—and in the second sport—the Seminoles won the title. Sanders's teammates celebrated. He went back to the team's hotel for some well-deserved sleep.

By Sanders's junior year in college, National Football League scouts were already touting him as a future first-round pick. Baseball scouts, too, believed he could make it in that sport. For his part, Sanders decided to try a third sport. Encouraged by his one race the year before, he joined the track team. He knew nothing about the techniques of sprinting, but he worked with Coach Roberts to improve his form. Quickly, he became a star. In the Metro Conference tournament, he won the 100-yard championship with a terrific time of 10.1 seconds. In the same tournament, he ran a 200-yard dash for the first time in his life and finished in 20.7 seconds. Not only was that fast enough to win the race; it was within one second of the world record. In addition to helping the Seminoles win the first-place trophy, Sanders took home the Most Valuable Player award. For once, he was modest. "It really wasn't something I thought I could do," he said.

On the football field, there was no modesty. Sanders had 46 tackles and 4 interceptions in his third football season. He ran back punts for 381 yards, a school record. The Seminoles went

11–1, finishing the year with a win in the Fiesta Bowl. Sanders was awarded the Jim Thorpe Trophy as the nation's top college defensive back.

Part of his talent was his gift of gab. Sanders would talk to the receivers playing against him, to try to throw them off their game. Once, for example, Sanders heard that Andre Rison of Michigan State University had called him "an average defensive back." So when the two teams played, Sanders kept a running war of words going with Rison. "I watched you on film and I thought you were great," Sanders told Rison. "The film must have lied." The psyche-out worked, as Rison had just one catch for 11 yards. Florida State won the game.

In June 1988 the New York Yankees used their thirtieth-round draft pick to take Deion Sanders, an outfielder from Fort Myers, Florida. The Yankees offered Sanders $428,000 for two years, and he jumped at it. The first thing he did with the money was buy his mom a new house. "Whatever I needed as a child, she made sure I had," he said. "Now I want to make sure she has whatever she needs."

He played 28 minor-league games that summer. He batted .284 and stole 14 bases. His manager said that if he stuck with baseball, he could become a star. But sticking to one sport was not Deion's plan.

That fall he started his final year as a college football player. It was his best season. The Seminoles again went 11–1, beating Auburn University to win the Sugar Bowl. Sanders had a last-minute interception to seal that game. For the season, he had 14 interceptions, tying a school record. He led all college punt

Deion Sanders answers reporters' questions at the press conference after he was called up to play for the New York Yankees. A few weeks prior, Sanders had been chosen fifth in the 1989 NFL Draft.

returners with a 15.2-yard average. He made every All-America team and won every award given to defensive backs.

There were highlights galore. Against Southern Mississippi, he picked off a Brett Favre pass on the game's second play and sprinted 39 yards for a touchdown. Against Clemson, he waited for a punt while standing next to the Clemson sideline. He bragged to his opponents that he would run the punt back all the way—and then he did it.

That was the year that Sanders invented his second nickname—Neon Deion—and tried to live up to it. He started wearing gaudy clothing and jewelry. He made up stories for eager reporters, who would write down every word as if it were gospel. He arrived for his final home game in a rented white stretch limo, and smiled as photographers snapped him standing next to it in a tuxedo.

"If he's around a crowd of writers he'll show off," Coach Bowden explained. "But by himself, he's very low-key and likable, and a very kind person."

The Sugar Bowl marked the end of Sanders's brilliant college career. He hoped, however, for one more shot. He asked Florida State basketball coach Pat Kennedy whether he could play in one game. "I'm a real crowd pleaser," Sanders promised. Kennedy declined the offer.

Basketball might say no to Sanders, but baseball surely could not. In the summer of 1989, the Yankees called him up to the majors, after just 62 minor-league games. "He can be anything he wants in baseball," said Buck Showalter, his manager in Columbus, Ohio. "All he needs is time."

Falcons owner Rankin Smith thought Sanders to be the player that he could build his entire franchise around.

Around the same time, the National Football League held its annual draft of college players. The Atlanta Falcons chose Sanders with the fifth pick in the first round. Falcons owner Rankin Smith said that Sanders could be the one player around whom the Falcons could build their entire franchise. Smith predicted that Sanders would be a great football player for a decade.

Yankees or Falcons? Baseball or football? Deion Sanders had a decision to make. Or did he?

Chapter

3

A Man With Many Talents

Millions of boys grow up playing baseball in America. As Little Leaguers, most dream—just a little—about someday playing in the majors. A child who is really talented may make his high school team. A high school star might get to play college ball. And only the best at that level go on to the minor leagues.

To make the majors? Well, the chances of ending up there are about one in one hundred thousand.

Similar odds exist in football. About one million youngsters play high school football each year. Just forty thousand or so get to play in college. And only about fifteen hundred players are in the National Football League in any given year.

After negotiating with the Falcons, Deion finally got the contract he wanted. It would let him play two sports.

To reach the top in one sport is an outstanding feat. To do so in two sports would seem impossible.

But that's where Deion Sanders was in the summer of 1989. His pro baseball career was going so well that the Yankees promoted him to New York on May 31. He stood in Yankee Stadium that night and stared at the monuments honoring Hall of Fame players and managers. "I couldn't believe it," Sanders said. "I'm thinking about Mickey Mantle and Babe Ruth and Lou Gehrig. I'm saying, 'I'm twenty-one years old and I'm really here.' "

The Atlanta Falcons wanted him to be in the NFL. They viewed Sanders as the most-important building block of their future. Baseball, the Falcons said, was just interfering with his progress in football.

Many so-called experts in both sports advised Sanders to focus on one or the other. Make a choice, they said. No man can succeed in two sports at the same time.

Actually, a few men had. The most famous was Jim Thorpe, who is considered to be the greatest American athlete of the twentieth century. Thorpe played seven years of both baseball and football. But the sports seasons were shorter back then. The physical demands were not as great.

More recently a few men tried two sports, but most wound up giving up one of them. For example, Danny Ainge was much better at basketball than baseball, so he quit playing baseball to star for the Boston Celtics. Brian Jordan was a fine defensive back for the Falcons, but he preferred baseball. So he left the

Deion Sanders scored a touchdown in his first NFL game! He became the first pro athlete to hit a home run and score a touchdown in the same week.

NFL in 1992 to focus on playing outfield for the St. Louis Cardinals.

The only recent athlete to star in two sports before Sanders was Bo Jackson, who became the first man to make the all-star teams in both Major League Baseball and the NFL. But Jackson injured his hip making a run for the Los Angeles Raiders in 1990. The injury forced him to retire.

Then came Deion Sanders. He was confused in the summer of 1989. He loved both sports and did not want to give up either one. Everyone told him to make a choice, but he figured, why not try both? The problem was that the baseball season runs into October, a month after the football season begins. After months of haggling, Sanders finally got the Falcons to agree to an unusual deal. The Falcons let him play out the entire baseball season and then join their football team with no practice.

So—at least for a few months—Sanders concentrated on baseball. He batted .281 and stole 33 bases for two of the Yankees' farm teams. Then, in May, the Yankees called him up. Standing in Yankee Stadium he told reporters, "You sprinkle a crowd around me and that's what I like. Then you'll see what I can do."

It did not take long. In the first inning of his first major-league game, Sanders threw out a Seattle Mariners runner from deep center field. Three innings later, he got his first major-league hit and drove in a run. Four days later, in Milwaukee County Stadium, he hit his first home run. He used his great speed to make several highlight-film catches.

His first stay in the majors was brief, just twelve days. It ended when the Yankees regular center fielder, Roberto Kelly, returned from an injury. The Yankees decided that Sanders would learn more by playing every day at the Triple-A level than just a few days a week in the big leagues. But they were impressed. "There's no doubt in my mind that Deion can be a major league star," boasted Yankees owner George Steinbrenner. "Sure, he makes mistakes, but those are of a learning-experience type. I've never seen a kid come in and do what he did."

Sanders viewed baseball and football very differently. He considered himself a star in football. He called himself Prime Time, and mugged for every camera he could find. In baseball, however, he was more modest. He thought of himself as just

The Atlanta Braves signed Sanders to be their starting left fielder in 1991. From left to right are Steve Avery, David Justice, Ron Gant, and Sanders.

another young prospect trying to make it in a tough sport. "I'm not Prime Time in baseball," he said. "One guy can't dominate around here."

Late that season, he was again called up to the Yankees for a short time. On September 5, he hit a home run against Jerry Reed of the Seattle Mariners. The next night, he struck out in his last at-bat of the season. He high-fived his teammates goodbye in the Yankees clubhouse. Then he caught a late-night flight to Atlanta. That was on a Wednesday. Four days later, with almost no practice, Deion Sanders made his pro football debut.

The Falcons had billed him as something special. Many fans and teammates did not know what to make of him. After all, he arrived in Atlanta and immediately told the television cameras, "Hello, Atlanta. This is Deion Sanders, Prime Time. It's five minutes to eight. The thrill is here." He showed up wearing enough gold jewelry to stock a store. In total, he was wearing four rings, two bracelets, a Gucci watch, and seven gold necklaces, including one that dangled a giant dollar sign. He wore dark sunglasses and custom-made spikes. In the Falcons locker room, he set up a CD player to blare a rap music song about himself—sung by himself.

Some fans, and a few players, did not appreciate his act. Football is a tough game played by tough men. They viewed Sanders as a loudmouth who had not proven anything in the NFL.

Maybe so. But that did not take too long.

On September 10, 1989, Sanders played in the Falcons home opener against the Los Angeles Rams. Five minutes into the game, he lined up to return his first punt. He dropped it, picked it up, and saw Rams tacklers quickly closing in. So he ran 12 yards backward to the Atlanta 20-yard line. As his own coach shook his head at what looked like a mistake, Sanders faked out three tacklers and started back upfield. He cut to his left to avoid two more tacklers. He then outran the few remaining Rams with a shot to catch him. In the end, his move was counted as a 68-yard punt return for a touchdown. In fact, Sanders probably covered more than 120 yards on the play.

Never before had an athlete hit a major-league home run and scored an NFL touchdown in the same week. But Sanders was no ordinary athlete. It isn't just that he was as fast as any other player in the league. He also has amazing acceleration. Most athletes need to run a few steps before they reach top speed, but Sanders seems to be at full throttle from his first step. When he got the ball, he was gone before anyone could touch him.

At six-feet one-inch and just 195 pounds, Sanders appeared tiny next to football's three-hundred-pound linemen. But he has always been fearless. As a rookie in 1989, he intercepted 5 passes for the Falcons. He quickly became recognized as one of the league's top defensive backs. He averaged 11 yards per punt return and nearly 21 yards per kickoff return. He made 39 tackles. He would have had more except that opposing quarterbacks were afraid to throw his way.

Overall, it was a great year for Sanders, but not for the Falcons. The team won just 3 of its 16 games. At season's end, Head Coach Jim Hanifan was fired, and he was replaced by Jerry Glanville. The new coach was a loud showman who appreciated Sanders's style. He also knew how to build a team. The Falcons improved to 5 wins in 1990 and 11 in 1991. That year, they made the playoffs for the first time in nine years. Sanders tied for the league lead with 6 interceptions. He was voted to start in the Pro Bowl, the NFL's all-star game. He intercepted another pass in that contest.

Coach Glanville liked Sanders not just as a defensive player, but also as an offensive threat. So the coach worked Sanders into the Falcons offense for a few plays every game. In 1991, Sanders was the only NFL player to do all of the following: catch a pass, intercept a pass, return a punt and a kickoff, and make tackles on defense and special teams. He was all over the football field.

Still, he felt unfulfilled. Speaking of his football success, he said, "I've accomplished that. Now it's time for me to accomplish a goal in baseball—enormous success. I'm a good baseball player. I can be a star baseball player."

Could he? After a promising start with the Yankees, things had gone sour in that area. Sanders hit just .158 with New York in 1990 and ended up being sent back to the minor leagues. When he joined the Falcons that fall, the Yankees cut him.

The Atlanta Braves, who at the time played baseball in the same stadium where the Falcons played football, decided to take a chance on the local speedster. In 1991, they signed him and named him their starting left fielder. Again, he had problems. Sanders could play the outfield and steal bases with the best of them, but he was not developing as a hitter. He batted just .191 in limited time with the Braves. By season's end he was playing for their minor-league club in Richmond, Virginia.

His goal was to star in two sports. He had come close—as close as any man other than Bo Jackson—but had fallen a little short. He decided then to give himself one more year. If he did not succeed in baseball in 1992, that would be the end of it. Deion Sanders was determined not to fail.

Chapter

4

An Athlete Who Excels

Deion Sanders began to approach baseball differently in 1992. He would not just work on running, hitting, and throwing. He decided to master the mental part of the game.

As he went through spring training with his new team, the Atlanta Braves, Sanders started keeping a book on opposing pitchers. After every at-bat he would write down notes: What were pitchers throwing him? What pitches were getting him out? How were other teams setting their defense against him?

"I've accomplished my goal in that other thing," he said, meaning pro football. "Now it's time for me to accomplish a goal in this thing." That, of course, meant baseball.

His best chance would come in 1992. Atlanta's regular center fielder, Otis Nixon, was under suspension for drug abuse.

Nixon would have to miss the start of the season. If Sanders could handle the starting job, it was his. Braves manager Bobby Cox gave him special attention in spring training. Cox changed his new player's batting stance, turning Sanders a bit more toward the pitcher. The move allowed Sanders to see the ball better, especially against left-handed pitchers. He had always had a tough time hitting lefties.

When the season started, Sanders was on fire. He got hits in 14 straight games. By the end of April, he was leading the National League with a .407 batting average. Critics thought he would fizzle out. Instead, he enjoyed the finest year of his baseball career. At season's end, he was still hitting .304. He stole 26 bases for the Braves, and he led the league with 14 triples. In fact, Los Angeles Dodgers manager Tommy Lasorda called

Deion definitely figured out the baseball "thing" in 1992. He led the major leagues in triples and hit over .300.

Sanders the most important offensive player on the Braves, even though their power-packed lineup included sluggers like Fred McGriff and David Justice. "Deion is aggressive," said Lasorda. "That's what makes their offense."

Sanders was also a part of the Braves clubhouse chemistry. His teammates liked his stories and his sense of humor. His best friend was pitcher Steve Avery. The two men were quite different—one a brash black man from Florida and the other a shy white man from Michigan. They called themselves the Two Musketeers and laughed about their differences. Once, for example, Avery grew so tired of Sanders making fun of his boring clothes that he handed his friend five thousand dollars and told him to shop for a new wardrobe. Sanders came back with bags full of new items. The next day, Avery was seen wearing a flowery shirt and mustard-colored pants. Teammates almost laughed the quiet Avery out of the clubhouse.

That fall, Sanders signed a new contract to play football for the Falcons. It was an unusual deal. Under its terms, he would give up baseball once the NFL season started—unless the Braves were in the pennant race. If that was the case, he would juggle between both Atlanta teams.

That's exactly what happened. In fact, the same night he signed his football contract, he arrived at Fulton County Stadium in Atlanta for a baseball game. With the score tied 2–2, he pinch ran for Lonnie Smith in the ninth inning. He raced to third on an error and then scored the winning run on a sacrifice fly by Ron Gant. "Whether Deion plays every day or not, he definitely contributes to this club," Braves shortstop Jeff Blauser said after the game.

As the Braves cruised toward the playoffs, the Falcons 1992 season was a disappointment. After winning 10 games plus a playoff game in 1991, they fell to just 6 wins. Sanders, however, had reached the All-Pro level. He broke a kickoff for a 99-yard touchdown in the first game against the Washington Redskins, but the Falcons lost, 24–17. In Chicago against the Bears he ran a kickoff back 55 yards, but the Falcons missed a field goal that would have won the game. He led the NFL in kickoff returns and shut down most receivers from his spot at cornerback.

Opposing players always looked to see where Sanders lined up at the start of each play. They tried to keep the ball away from him. Fans also closely followed his actions. "He may be the fastest person I've ever seen on a football field," said 49ers defensive back Merton Hanks.

At season's end, he was the leader in the Pro Bowl balloting done by players and coaches. They voted him in at both cornerback and kick returner. League rules said that he could only start at one position, so he took his spot on defense.

Doing two things at once seemed only natural to Sanders. The ultimate test came in October 1992.

That season, the Braves faced the Pittsburgh Pirates in the National League Championship Series (NLCS). On October 10, a Saturday, Sanders played in a night game for the Braves. He struck out in his only at-bat. He then announced that the next day, he would try a two-sport doubleheader—football in the afternoon, baseball at night. The only problem was that the

Deion Sanders talks with Barry Bonds of the Pittsburgh Pirates before Game 4 of the 1992 NLCS. Later that day, he flew to Miami to play football against the Dolphins.

Falcons football game was in Florida and the Braves baseball game was in Pittsburgh—fifteen hundred miles apart.

Not everyone thought this was a great idea. Some fans questioned his loyalty to the Braves, who needed the win to get into the World Series. Braves general manager John Schuerholz worried that Sanders would get injured playing football. But Sanders's teammates understood. "Deion has to do what he has to do," said Avery.

As Sanders explained it, he was getting the chance to live every little boy's fantasy. "This is the kind of thing kids dream about," he said. "In the morning, they're Michael Jordan on the basketball court. In the afternoon, they're Deion Sanders on the football field. I'm a kid still."

So, at 1:15 A.M., after that Saturday night baseball game, Sanders boarded a jet for Florida. He slept as the jet flew south. He landed at Fort Lauderdale-Hollywood Airport with the sun still below the horizon and headed to the Falcons hotel for a few more hours of sleep. Then, at 11:00 a.m., he joined his Falcons teammates at Joe Robbie Stadium for a game against the Miami Dolphins.

Sanders entered the game at 1:01 p.m. He returned two kickoffs for 42 yards and one punt for another 7 yards. He played a steady game at cornerback. He even entered the game on offense, catching a 9-yard pass. The Falcons led, 17–7, in the third quarter, but eventually lost to the Dolphins, 21–17.

After the game, trainers hooked Sanders up to a saline drip to replace his lost body fluids. He spent a few minutes with teammates. Then he limped off to catch a flight. He ate on the plane, took a nap as it flew over the Carolinas and landed in Pittsburgh an hour before Game 5 of the NLCS. A private helicopter whisked him to the stadium. He arrived just a few minutes before game time. He changed into his baseball uniform as the national anthem played.

After all the buildup, Braves manager Bobby Cox did not use Sanders that night. Some believed Cox viewed Sanders's day as just a publicity stunt. But the Braves won the pennant, and Cox put Sanders on the World Series roster against the Toronto Blue Jays.

And what a World Series he had. Sanders shared time with Ron Gant in the outfield. He played in four of the six games and

Sanders was traded to the Cincinnati Reds early in the 1994 season. Here, he shows off a smooth homerun swing.

batted .533, with 8 hits in 15 at-bats. He stole 5 bases and scored 4 runs. His best moment came in Game 5. The Braves were down three games to one and facing elimination. In the fifth inning, Sanders came to bat against Blue Jays ace Jack Morris. The score was tied, 2–2, and Otis Nixon was on second base. Morris had used curveballs to get Sanders out twice earlier in the game. This time, however, he threw a fastball. Sanders smashed it into center field to score Nixon with the go-ahead run. Three batters later, he scored on a grand slam by Lonnie Smith that broke open the game.

In Game 6, Sanders singled, doubled, scored a run, and stole 2 bases. He even threw out a Blue Jays runner attempting to score. It wasn't enough, however. The Braves lost in extra innings, ending the World Series. Afterward, his Braves teammates said good-bye in the clubhouse and went off to relax through the winter. Sanders, of course, went back to Atlanta. He had a football game to play that weekend.

Sanders ended up enjoying his best year yet in professional sports in 1992. It ended, however, on a sad note. Early in 1993, his father died of a brain tumor. Mims Sanders had left home when Deion was a young boy, and the two rarely saw each other. But when Deion Sanders became an adult, they became close friends. Sanders took his father's death very hard. He began a ritual that he practiced until he retired. Every time he got on base in baseball or scored in football, he tapped his chest and pointed to the sky. That is his way of honoring his father.

Sanders had solid seasons in both sports in 1993. *Baseball America* magazine even chose him as the top base runner in the

National League and the second most exciting player, behind Barry Bonds. Again, the Braves won their division. They lost an exciting National League Championship Series to the Philadelphia Phillies.

But the Braves grew weary of the two-sport shuffle. Early in the 1994 season, Atlanta traded him to the Cincinnati Reds for another outfielder, Roberto Kelly. That was the same player that Sanders had replaced when he made his first major-league start for the Yankees. With the Reds, Sanders hit .277 in 46 games, scored 26 runs, and stole 19 bases.

For Sanders, Cincinnati was a new town, and his third baseball team in five years. It meant making many new adjustments. Of course, as a professional athlete, Sanders was used to new places. Soon, he would find a new home for himself in football as well. And that change would be even more dramatic, for Sanders, and for the entire National Football League.

Deion Sanders's life changed dramatically in 1994. He started the baseball season with the Atlanta Braves and finished with the Cincinnati Reds. He planned to keep playing football for the Atlanta Falcons, but that would change, too.

The Falcons grew tired of Sanders's two-sport juggling act. Also, they were having a tough time affording his high salary. So in the summer of 1994, they decided not to offer him a new contract. That made Sanders a free agent. He could sign with any NFL team that wanted him—and could afford him. And there were a lot of interested clubs.

Chapter 5

Career Change

That summer, Sanders filmed a commercial for a new video game that he would star in. The ad's producers wanted to be sure they had Sanders in the uniform of his next NFL club. So they filmed separate versions, with him wearing the outfits of the Cowboys, Dolphins, Eagles, 49ers, Broncos, and Saints.

Each club wanted the NFL's top cornerback. The New Orleans Saints made the best offer—$17 million for four seasons. But something else was more important to Sanders than money at this time. He wanted to play for a winner. He wanted to get to the Super Bowl. "Forget finances," he told reporters. "I'm knocking on the door of a dream."

So he chose the San Francisco 49ers. The Niners knew how good Sanders was from playing the Falcons twice each season.

And they were among the NFL's best teams. They had fallen one game short of the Super Bowl the two previous years by losing to the Dallas Cowboys. Both times, Cowboys receiver Michael Irvin had burned San Francisco's defensive backs. Sanders, the Niners hoped, would push them past Dallas.

San Francisco offered him less money than other teams did. They also offered just a one-year contract. It was risky for Sanders. If he suffered a career-ending injury, it would mean the loss of millions of dollars. But Sanders did not hesitate. "I'm going to win a Super Bowl here," he said. "That ring is the most important thing."

In some ways it was a strange fit. The Niners were a conservative club. They were not known for flash or sass. How would this high-stepping, chain-wearing bigmouth fit in?

Sanders knew that some players and fans in San Francisco were worried that he might upset team chemistry. So he went to his teammates on the first day and told them how much he wanted to fit in. And he dedicated himself to working hard and studying film in order to become a better player.

"We had all heard a lot about Deion and his style and you wonder about a guy like that," said teammate Bart Oates. "He was different, though. In just a few days you could see that the gold chains and talk were just for entertainment. Underneath all that, he was quite a nice guy. I never saw anyone who worked so hard. He truly wanted us to go to the Super Bowl and worked like a dog."

From the start, Sanders was the extra ingredient that the Niners needed. He saved a win in the season opener against the

Deion Sanders signed with the San Francisco 49ers prior to the 1994 NFL season. He felt they were a Super Bowl contender.

Saints. The Niners held a 17–13 lead with a minute left. The Saints were driving for the winning touchdown. But when Saints quarterback Jim Everett threw a deep pass, Sanders stepped out of nowhere to intercept it. He raced 76 yards down the sideline for a touchdown, to put the game out of reach.

The next week, the Niners faced Sanders's old team, the Falcons. Sanders had looked forward to playing against his old friends and teammates, but the Falcons resented Sanders and started trash-talking. "Deion going to San Francisco might be one of the best things that ever happened to this team," said Falcons wide receiver Andre Rison. "People acted as if Deion was our savior."

The words stung Sanders. So did the Atlanta fans who booed him as he stepped onto the field to start the game. Sanders did not say hello to his old teammates during warm-ups. Now he wanted nothing to do with them.

The game started well for the Niners. They were up 21–3 in the first quarter. Sanders was shutting down Rison, who was his assignment for the day. Then Rison went out on a deep pattern, and the two players started bumping each other. Bumps turned into shoves. As the referee blew the whistle, the two old friends stood at midfield, slapping each other in a furious fight that lasted several minutes.

Surprisingly, neither player was thrown out of the game. But Sanders was even angrier than before. He wanted revenge against Rison, against other Falcons, and against the fans who had booed him. Late in the second quarter he got his chance. He intercepted a pass from Atlanta quarterback Jeff George near his own goal line by stepping in front of a receiver. As he began to race down the sideline, he ran past the Falcons bench sideways, pointing at former teammates. With 40 yards to go, he looked up at the fans and began high-stepping. In the end, he took the ball 93 yards for a touchdown. It was the longest interception return of his career.

The season kept going well. The 49ers finished the regular season at 13–3, the best record in the NFL. Sanders had 6 interceptions, 3 of which he returned for touchdowns. The Niners knew they did not have to worry about his side of the field because he could cover any receiver one-on-one. The writers who cover the NFL voted him the league's Defensive Player of the Year.

Sanders faced his former team, the Atlanta Falcons, in the second game of the 1994 season. He returned an interception 93 yards for a touchdown. The 49ers would destroy the Falcons that day, 42-3.

For the third straight season, the Niners faced the Cowboys in the National Football Conference title game. The winner would play in Super Bowl XXIX. The Cowboys had won the last two title matchups, but this time, San Francisco had its new weapon.

The Niners decided to have Sanders cover Cowboys receiver Alvin Harper one-on-one. Two other defensive backs would double-team Dallas star Michael Irvin. A year earlier, Harper had crushed the 49ers with a 70-yard touchdown catch. But not this year. In sixty minutes of football, Harper had just one catch for 14 yards. Sanders intercepted a pass, meaning that he had as many catches as the man he was covering. The 49ers won, 38–28, and headed for the Super Bowl in Miami.

Sanders showed up in Miami with three watches. Why? Simple, he explained. One for each time zone: Eastern, Pacific, and Prime Time.

As always, he was flashy and funny. But there is another side to Deion Sanders. Under the gold jewelry, the dazzling shades, and the big mouth, he is a solid citizen and a loyal friend. He does not smoke or drink. He fines himself fifty dollars every time he uses a curse word. His bedtime during the season was 10:00 p.m., suggesting that away from the spotlight, he is more Nap Time than Prime Time.

Sanders has five children; two from his first marriage, and three from his second. In 1996, he and his wife, Carolyn, split up. That was tremendously upsetting to Sanders. He rededicated himself to his church and to leading a righteous

"Prime Time" is shown taking down Chargers running back Natrone Means during Super Bowl XXIX. He picked off a pass later in the game, and won his first NFL title.

life. He eventually remarried, but filed for divorce again in 2011 ending their thirteen-year union.

Sure, he loves money and material things. He bought a $250,000 Lamborghini Diablo as a gift to himself for making the Super Bowl in 1994. And he owned an eighty-five-acre estate outside Atlanta. The house had its own football field, baseball field, full-sized basketball court, and miniature golf course. But if you ask him what is really important, he'll say that it is his children.

"I don't want to be known as anything else in life but a great father," he said.

Actually, there are a few other dreams. Sanders built the Prime Time Kids Center. At this youth center in Atlanta, Georgia, boys and girls can get help doing their homework and play many different sports—the activity, he says, that kept him out of trouble as a child. "It would have been easy for me to sell drugs," he said. "But I had practice. My friends who didn't have practice, they went straight to the streets and never left."

His other dream was to become a recording artist. In 1995, Sanders recorded an album called *Prime Time*. One of its songs was entitled "Respect Your Woman." The words were great, but, to be honest, Sanders was a terrible singer. The album was re-released in 2005 as *The Encore Remix*.

As a football player? That was something else. More than 130 million TV viewers watched Sanders and the Niners take on the San Diego Chargers in Super Bowl XXIX on January 29, 1995. The game was a blowout from the start. San Francisco scored on the third play of the game, a 44-yard pass from Steve

Young to Jerry Rice. Niners running back Ricky Watters scored 3 touchdowns. Sanders did not really get tested, because the 49ers defensive line kept Chargers quarterback Stan Humphries on the run.

Late in the fourth quarter, Sanders picked off a Humphries pass 2 yards into his own end zone. His eyes grew wide. He thought he could return it 102 yards for a touchdown, but he made it just to his own 22 before being tackled.

The Niners won the game, 49–26. It was a special moment for Sanders, who became the first man ever to play in both the World Series and the Super Bowl. His dream had come true.

A few months after the dream, there was major news. Sanders had signed just a one-year deal with San Francisco, meaning that he was again a free agent. One team that could not afford him was the 49ers. They were too squeezed by the salary cap the NFL places on its clubs.

Sanders had to go shopping for a new football team again. There would be no shortage of interested clubs. But which would be the right fit?

Chapter 6

Still Going Strong

In 1995, Deion Sanders again switched baseball teams. That July, the Cincinnati Reds traded him to the San Francisco Giants in a seven-player deal. Sanders played center field and batted leadoff for the Giants. A sprained ankle slowed him for much of the season. Still, he batted .285 and finished third in the National League in triples.

The baseball trade led to an obvious question: Would Sanders become San Francisco's two-sport star with the Giants and the 49ers? Sanders said he liked the city. But as a free agent in the National Football League, he could again field offers from all interested teams.

It didn't take long for one team to step forward. Dallas Cowboys owner Jerry Jones offered Sanders an amazing $35 million deal for seven years. It included a $13 million bonus, to be paid the minute Sanders signed his name to the contract. How could he say no?

What a match it was. The Cowboys—unlike the 49ers—were a loud, brash team. Their players liked to taunt opponents and perform victory dances. None of that offended Sanders. He said that "America's Team," as the Cowboys were called, needed "America's player." He even said he liked playing with a star on his helmet.

The Cowboys roster boasted great players such as running back Emmitt Smith, quarterback Troy Aikman, and wide receiver Michael Irvin. They had already won two Super Bowls in the 1990s. "Welcome to the galaxy of stars," Dallas assistant coach Joe Avezzano said when Sanders first showed up in the locker room. "Deion fits right in, doesn't he?"

After taking a few games off to let his aching ankle heal, Deion Sanders began his career with the Cowboys on October 29, 1995, against his old team, the Atlanta Falcons. He did not dominate the game, but he fit right in. Falcons quarterback Jeff George completed just one pass against him, an 11-yard toss to Bert Emanuel. The Cowboys won, 28–13, at the Georgia Dome. "Defensively, I threw a one-hitter," he said afterward. "I'll take that any day."

The following week, the Cowboys beat the Philadelphia Eagles, 34–12. In that game, Sanders intercepted a pass at the end of the first half. In the second half, he took a reverse handoff from Kevin Williams on a punt return and scampered 43 yards to set up a field goal.

And things just kept getting better. With Sanders on board, the Cowboys breezed through the regular season with 12 wins and just 4 losses. They trounced the Eagles in the playoffs, 30–11, as Sanders came in on offense and ran a reverse for a 21-yard touchdown. They beat the Green Bay Packers, 38–27, to get to the Super Bowl. In that game, Sanders shut down dangerous Packers receiver Robert Brooks. On offense, he chipped in with a key 35-yard, third-down pass reception.

That win put the Cowboys into Super Bowl XXX against the Pittsburgh Steelers, played on January 28, 1996. Again, Sanders was given the job of covering the other team's toughest receiver. This time, he held Yancey Thigpen to 3 catches for 19 yards. In fact, Sanders produced more yards on offense than he allowed

After one season with the 49ers, Sanders signed with the Dallas Cowboys. Sanders would be perhaps best remembered for his time in Dallas.

on defense. Early in the game, he hauled in a 47-yard bomb from Aikman to set up the Cowboys' first touchdown. Sanders and his teammates celebrated a 27–17 win over Pittsburgh. It was Sanders's second straight Super Bowl victory.

Sanders would later say that 1995 was his favorite season in pro football. For the second straight year he was an All-Pro selection and played in the Pro Bowl in Honolulu. But he wanted more from the sport, so in 1996, he decided to dedicate himself entirely to football. He retired from baseball—although he said he might later change his mind. He rested during the spring, worked out through the summer, and came to Cowboys camp early. It was time, he said, to ". . . get down. Do my thing. Get busy. Do the ultimate. They're going to have to put seat belts in the stadium."

The ultimate, as he saw it, was playing both ways. Sanders had dabbled at playing wide receiver over the years. In his first seven seasons, he caught 18 passes, including 2 for touchdowns. But in 1996, Dallas coach Barry Switzer asked Sanders to consider playing offense full-time. The Cowboys had lost wide receiver Alvin Harper as a free agent a year earlier. Now other clubs were double-teaming Irvin, Dallas's top receiver. The Cowboys needed another offensive threat.

He would still play defensive back under Switzer's plan. After all, Sanders was considered the best cover cornerback in the NFL. Switzer was asking Sanders to try something that no pro football player had done in years—play on both sides of the ball in every game. Typically, there are about 120 plays in each football game. Coach Switzer wanted Sanders to be on the field for at least ninety of those plays.

Wouldn't Sanders get too tired to cover other teams' receivers?

"I know that a lot of coaches and offensive coordinators in this league will be sitting back and smiling because of what we're doing," Switzer said. But Sanders would be sure to draw double coverage, the coach figured. That would give Irvin more room and also open up the running game for Emmitt Smith.

The plan worked. Playing in more than half of Dallas's offensive plays in 1996, Sanders caught 36 passes. His 475

In 1996, Cowboys head coach Barry Switzer asked Sanders to play both offense and defense. Deion did almost everything on the football field: running the ball, catching the ball, defending, and returning kicks.

receiving yards were second on the club. He was as good as ever on defense. He intercepted just two passes during the season, but that was because the other team almost never threw the ball in his direction. And he led the team with 3 fumble recoveries. Again he was chosen to start at cornerback for the National Football Conference Pro Bowl squad—his fifth selection in eight NFL seasons.

There were many highlights during the season. Sanders's best two-way game may have been a Monday night contest against the Eagles late in September. In the second quarter, he picked off his first pass of the season, reaching over his shoulder to snare a bomb attempt by Philadelphia quarterback Rodney Peete. That set up a field goal, putting Dallas ahead, 17–10. Then, on the Cowboys' next offensive series he caught a 39-yard pass from Aikman to set up another touchdown. That one put the game away, as the *Monday Night Football* announcers sang Sanders's praises. In all, he had 7 tackles, 5 pass receptions, and the interception that night. He played in 108 of 121 plays in the game—and then collapsed in the locker room. Who could blame him for being exhausted?

The Cowboys' season ended in January with a playoff loss to the Carolina Panthers. Sanders went home. He relaxed by going fishing for two months. Then he decided to give baseball one more try.

The Cincinnati Reds wanted Sanders back for 1997. They offered him a one-year contract. Truth was, however, they were nervous. How would he play after a full year away from the sport? Could he return to his old form at age twenty-nine?

Deion Sanders gives his enshrinement speech after being inducted into the Pro Football Hall of Fame.

Sanders was determined to be better than ever. He spent hour after hour working on his skills. He hired a private coach to teach him the art of drag bunting. And he shortened his batting stroke to cut down on strikeouts.

It all worked. "I was shocked," said Reds catcher Joe Oliver. "He took a year off and actually improved. I don't know how you do that."

Sanders batted .273 in 1997 and played a steady center field. His 56 stolen bases were second best in the National League. He was leading in steals by almost a dozen when he left the Reds in September to go back to the NFL.

And so it was, as pro sports' miracle man went from sport to sport. Sanders's 1997 football season with the Cowboys was a disappointment. He broke a few ribs late in the season, and the Cowboys failed to make the NFL playoffs. Still, he was again named to play in the Pro Bowl in recognition of his outstanding talents.

His career continued through 1999 with the Dallas Cowboys before playing one season for the Washington Redskins. Prior to the 2000 season, he signed a 7-year, $56 million contract with the Redskins. He then retired after the 2000 season, but came out of retirement to play two seasons with the Baltimore Ravens from 2004 to 2005. After the 1997 season, he did not play baseball again until 2001 when he played his final season of professional baseball with the Cincinnati Reds.

Deion Sanders's athletic feats may never be duplicated. He was a star in two pro sports. He excelled at many positions on the football field. He played in the Super Bowl and the World

Series. And he helped two teams—the San Francisco 49ers and Dallas Cowboys—win NFL titles.

Sanders also became a very wealthy man. He combined his athletic talents and powerful personality to become a fan favorite. That brought dozens of TV commercials and ad campaigns. When he retired from football he became an NFL TV analyst for CBS. He has also worked as an NFL analyst for the NFL Network. In 2008, Sanders and his then-wife Pilar starred in their own reality show, *Deion & Pilar: Prime Time Love.*

Deion Sanders was inducted into the Pro Football Hall of Fame with the Class of 2011. In his speech he thanked nearly a hundred people and used it as an opportunity to motivate others. Sanders said, "This game, this game, this game, this game, this game taught me how to be a man. This game taught me if I could get knocked down, I've got to get my butt back up again. This game taught me there are things in life you can't do prematurely. They call it offsides. In life, it's just life."

Certainly, Sanders is someone special. Off the field, he supports charity efforts such as bringing holiday presents to sick children. After Hurricane Katrina in 2005, Sanders raised a large amount of money to help those affected. And in 2012, he co-founded a Dallas-area charter school, saying that he would also coach its football team. He loves the limelight, too. Deion Sanders boasts that he is the greatest bass fisherman in the world. Don't be surprised if he becomes a star in the coaching ranks as well.

Career Statistics

YEAR	TEAM	G	INT	YDS	KR	YDS	YPR	PR	YDS	YPR	TD
1989	Falcons	15	5	52	35	725	20.7	28	307	11.0	1
1990	Falcons	16	3	153	39	851	21.8	29	250	8.6	3
1991	Falcons	15	6	119	26	576	22.2	21	170	8.1	2
1992	Falcons	13	3	105	40	1,067	26.7	13	41	3.2	3
1993	Falcons	11	7	91	7	169	24.1	2	21	10.5	1
1994	49ers	14	6	303	0	0	0	0	0	0	3
1995	Cowboys	9	2	34	1	15	15.0	1	54	54.0	0
1996	Cowboys	16	2	3	0	0	0	1	4	4.0	2
1997	Cowboys	13	2	81	1	18	18.0	33	407	12.3	2
1998	Cowboys	11	5	153	1	16	16.0	24	375	15.6	3
1999	Cowboys	14	3	2	4	87	21.8	30	344	11.5	1
2000	Redskins	16	4	91	1	-1	-1.0	25	185	7.4	0
2001	DID NOT PLAY										
2002	DID NOT PLAY										
2003	DID NOT PLAY										
2004	Ravens	9	3	87	0	0	0	5	41	8.2	1
2005	Ravens	16	2	57	0	0	0	0	0	0	0
Career Totals		188	53	1,331	155	3,523	22.7	212	2,199	10.4	22

G = Games
INT = Interceptions
YDS = Yards
KR = Kick Returns
YPR = Yards per Return
PR = Punt Returns
TD= Touchdowns

More Info

Contact Deion Sanders

http://www.facebook.com/DeionSanders21

Twitter: @DeionSanders

http://www.deionsanders21.com/contact/

On the Internet at:

http://www.pro-football-reference.com/players/S/SandDe00.htm

http://www.baseball-reference.com/players/s/sandede02.shtml

Index